IDEAL Lucy
goes to the pool

Written by Kirt & Crystal Heap
Illustrated by Amber Leigh Luecke

Published by Lilly Bug Books via Kindle Direct Publishing

Written by Kirt & Crystal Heap

Illustrated by Amber Leigh Luecke
www.amberleighluecke.com

Copyright 2019 by Kirt & Crystal Heap
dba Lilly Bug Books

ISBN 9781694551320

All rights reserved. No part of this publication may be reproduced, stored digitally or transmitted in any form by any means electronic, mechanical, photocopying or otherwise without the prior permission of the authors.

Dedication

To our daughter Lillian Rosa Heap,

May you live your fullest life and accomplish all your dreams.

We love you now and forever.

-Love Mom and Dad

**Lilly is a happy bouncy little chick ready to go for a swim.
She's eager to splash and play all day.**

So eager she forgot to look both ways before trying to cross the road.

**"That's not ideal Lil,"
said Lilly's Dada holding her back.**

"It is ideal Lil to look both ways before crossing the road," said Mama.

And they all crossed the road safely.

After crossing the road Lilly was finally at the pool.
She was so excited she started to run.

Lilly's Mama sees her starting to run and says "That's not ideal Lil. You shouldn't run on slippery surfaces."

Lilly wanted to do a sweet cannonball into the pool.

So she cut to the front of the diving board line.

"That's not ideal Lil," said Dada
helping Lilly to the back of the line.
"It is ideal to wait your turn and share the fun."

**After waiting her turn
Lilly did a sweet cannonball into the pool!**

Lilly was getting cold and tired from all the swimming. She was ready to go home. She suddenly realized she forgot her towel and was really cold!

Lilly had an idea and asked Duckie if she could share his towel to dry off.

"That is certainly ideal Lil" said Duckie.
"I'll always share with a friend."

After drying off Lilly said thank you to Duckie and waved goodbye to all her friends.

Lilly had an **IDEAL** day at the pool.

Copyright 2019

Made in the USA
Columbia, SC
17 May 2021